Prairie Dog Rescue

by Christine Ricci

illustrated by Ron Zalme

Ready-to-Read

Simon Spotlight/Nick Jr.
New York   London   Toronto   Sydney

Based on the TV series *Nick Jr. Go, Diego, Go!*™ as seen on Nick Jr.®

SIMON SPOTLIGHT
An imprint of Simon & Schuster Children's Publishing Division
1230 Avenue of the Americas, New York, New York 10020

Manufactured in the United States of America
First Edition
2 4 6 8 10 9 7 5 3 1
Cataloging-in-Publication Data is available for this title from the Library of Congress.
ISBN-13: 978-1-4169-3363-2
ISBN-10: 1-4169-3363-8

Hi! I am 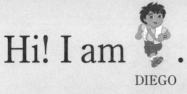.

DIEGO

I am on the prairie

with Mama  and

PRAIRIE DOG

Papa .

PRAIRIE DOG

live underground

PRAIRIE DOGS

in a .

BURROW

They can hide there if

they are in danger.

Oh, no!

I think I hear a !
COYOTE

are afraid of !
PRAIRIE DOGS   COYOTES

Mama  and

PRAIRIE DOG

Papa  need our help.

PRAIRIE DOG

We have to get their five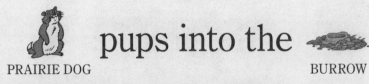

PRAIRIE DOG pups into the BURROW

to keep them safe from

the COYOTE.

There are lots of
animals on the prairie.
I see an and an .

ARMADILLO   OWL

Do you see any pups?
PRAIRIE DOG

Look! Two pups
PRAIRIE DOG

are eating .
GRASS

The is getting closer!

COYOTE

We need to find the other

 pups.

PRAIRIE DOG

We need to call them.

Say "Yip, yip!"

Two more pups

PRAIRIE DOG

heard our call.

They are jumping and

barking.

We need to carry

the pups.
PRAIRIE DOG

My can turn
RESCUE PACK

into anything I need.

Should we use a ,
BOAT

, or a to carry
SKIS   WAGON

the pups?
PRAIRIE DOG

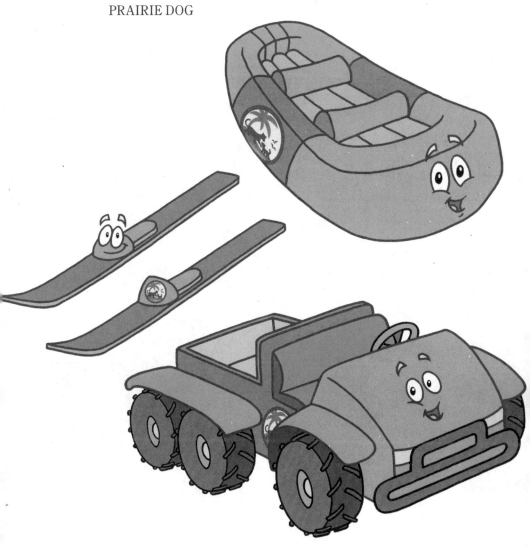

Yes! A  !
WAGON

How many  pups

PRAIRIE DOG

have we found?

One, two, three, four.

We need to find five

 pups.

PRAIRIE DOG

One is still missing.

We need to use

my to look
SPOTTING SCOPE

for the last pup.
PRAIRIE DOG

Do you see him?

There he is!

Oh, no!

The  is getting closer
COYOTE

to the pup.
PRAIRIE DOG

Which path should the 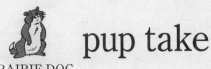 pup take to get to our  ?

PRAIRIE DOG

WAGON

Hooray!

We found all five pups.

PRAIRIE DOG

 **PRAIRIE DOGS** put a big pile

of at their  so
DIRT **BURROW**

they know where it is.

Do you see the biggest

pile of 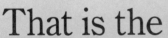?
DIRT

That is the !
BURROW

Mama and

PRAIRIE DOG

Papa

PRAIRIE DOG

are so happy to see all of

their  pups.

PRAIRIE DOG

Look!

Here comes the COYOTE !

We have to hurry.

All of the **PRAIRIE DOGS**

are safe inside the .
BURROW

The is gone.
COYOTE

Rescue complete!